GORY GAMES

FABULA METUS

ARIB UMAR

ISBN 979-888546043-9

Contents

Disclaimer

The story, all names, characters, and incidents portrayed in this production are fictitious. No identification with actual persons (living or deceased), places, buildings, and products is intended or should be inferred.

CHAPTER ONE

Last Trip

Hello everyone, my name is Raj and I was

Working in Mumbai. This is a story about when I was coming to Mumbai. whenever I remember this incident I was Goosebumps.

It was the time of 2008. I was living in a village .that is about 2000 km from Mumbai. At 9 o clock, I was started my journey. with my friend and we planned to stop in a hotel for this night we covered about 800 km distance from my village and started looking for a hotel. At late night we found a small hotel on the alone highway. My friend was telling me to stay here so we parked his car near the hotel and we came out and started looking around. Suddenly the gate open and we started looking towards the hotel gate somebody is coming to us. We look that a man with a candle in his hand coming to us. My friend asked him "can we stay here?" he didn't reply to us I asked him with a bold sound can we stay here

He stare at me and said come in

When we enter the hotel a boy attend us and said sir my name is Raghu you room will ready in a few minutes

And he start walking towards a corridor he suddenly turn and say sir did you want anything to eat we replied with no. We waiting in a lobby. Sudden light started dimming. It take a few seconds to cover with dark a smooth sound came to us sir your room is ready to come here we started walking slowly in his side when we reached our room. I look toward my watch

It was 2 o clock

I told him to rest I also lie down on the bed and try to sleep after an hour my friend has slept but I watch out someone was staring at us from a small window. I

got up from bed and tried to see his face but its face is covered with his hair I screamed and try to wake up my friend when he woke he said what happens

but I very scared

With finger

Pointed to the window when he looks window side

Nothing was on it he said that I am tired I forced him to leave this hotel

After some argument he finally agree to leave this hotel we slowly started moving towards the car a sound came to us

Wait where are you going now we ignored this sound and run towards the car

As we sit in the car I look at the hotel gate a woman with walking with her hand and saying hold on my friend looked at his eyes and started opening the gate of the car but I started driving the car. A few seconds we were at the highway I look in the mirror she was following us so fast .in few seconds she come near us and started laughing

Suddenly my friend start to stare at him and he was Strangling himself. I fast drive and do not stop in between the way.

My friend Fainted and after a couple of days in the hospital, he came to his senses.

After this incident, we never talk about this

CHAPTER TWO

Why did you come to my house?

Aishwarya and Uday going to be married was seven years his marriage anniversary is coming so uday planned a surprise party.

On the anniversary day, Uday covered Aishwarya eyes and came out from the city. when they arrived she was surprised she was in front of a big villa

which had a nameplate bearing his name

He looked at Uday in surprise Uday said that he wanted to buy a house for Aishwarya for a long time. But due to lack of money, that was not possible, when Uday heard about the Bhuvan bungalow from someone, he got it cheaply.

The span of his years is over, she hugged Uday loudly she did not know that he is thinking of his dream palace, she is going to ruin his life.

Uday or Aishwarya went inside the house. Everything was going well for a week and the two lived very happily in the house.

But after that Uday has to go out of India for a business conference.

Now Aishwarya was alone in her house, she liked the roof of her house very much, she used to sit on the swing on the roof all day and read the book. One night when she was sitting on the swing after eating food, suddenly she saw that a small child came out of one corner of the terrace and run towards the ladder, he felt that he had a sense of mind.

But then suddenly while swinging the swing, he felt a push from the back, he felt as if some supernatural power was trying to make him fall like a swing. He was getting a little worried now. She thought of going back down, as soon as she reached towards the door of the terrace, she heard the sound of a child running away from her feet, this time she was very scared after hearing that voice. It turned vertically and then the swing started to move slowly as if someone was sitting on it shaking or after seeing Ashwariya lowered her

Ran into the bedroom and Uday started calling but Uday was not picking up the phone, then when he started calling again, the network of the phone went to him only then he gets the room. The door opened on its own and a child started peeping into the room from outside the door, his face was frightening. Certain looks were displayed again. When she turned to find her phone. Suddenly the child stood in front of him. Some smoke came out of the child's mouth and went inside Aishwarya, then she became unconscious.

A few days later

When Uday came back to his house, he did not listen to Aishwarya and told her that she must have had a dream and you were very scared, all this is the result of reading your ghost book. You rest now, said this or went to the terrace, at that time he was about to leave midnight, suddenly he heard some sound from Aishwarya's room, he went downstairs in a hurry He saw that Aishwarya was hanging in the air and her voice had changed, she was shouting and saying that you get out of here, this is my house. Uday shouted and start reading

Bible's line then Aishwarya suddenly fall on bed Uday calls her friend and said come to my house with a priest.

The next day

His friend and a priest came into his house and they start moving towards Aishwarya room. When they open the gate of the room they are all startled. Aishwarya floating on and air eating a cat .when Aishwarya looked toward the priest. She start running with a hand his face is scary and his mouth was full of blood. The priest start moving towards him and said who are you? she replied I am Joe it is my house leave it no so I will kill you priest said loudly come down she came down and said it is my house priest asked him how?

she said that my father purchase this house on my birthday and we were living here very happily but after someday a man with his wife came and claim this house police throw my parents outside from the house but I stuck inside the couple who claimed this house is his. They killed me for becoming rich using black magic then Uday run away from this house and towards a cottage that is nearby his Bhuvan villa they called her parents to go with him and finally Joe met with her parents.

Not every but some stories will end with happiness.

CHAPTER THREE

LATE-NIGHT ONLINE

it was 2:25 AM i sat at my laptop aimlessly scrolling as the minutes dragged by only three more hours left until i needed to start getting ready for a long day of work i leaned back in my chair and cracked my neck as i heard the tension being released i contemplated crawling into my bed and calling in a night but my over stimulated brain was still rushing after several hours of scrolling through endless tweets half-reading reedit posts and hitting the next recommended video on YouTube i eventually found myself in the deadly cycle of switching between the home page and the inbox page on Facebook I reached across the table and took a long swig of my now flat Pepsi then lurched as i felt a trickle running down my chin and onto my exposed keyboard quickly using the sleeve of my hoodie i frantically wiped off the keys that the sugary liquid splashed onto i really need to stop snacking at my computer i thought to myself as i observed the many crumbs scattered between the keys don't judge me I'm sure you have done it too after looking over my somewhat cleaner keyboard with satisfaction i looked back onto the screen a massive jumble of letters were strewn across the Google search bar as a result of my late night keyboard scrubbing session i briefly considered goggling my own name for the third time that night but then decided that those three hours of sleep might be just enough to get me through my next eight hours shift as i was about to stand up a small square suddenly appeared in the corner of my screen it was plain white with a red frame with the bold letters flashing from blue to red reading this link will disappear in 60 seconds below a small timer began counting down from 60 to 59 to 58 nice try probably some low budget website or internet scam trying to trick me into taking their surveys or giving out my credit card information so that i can win that free new iPad the numbers counted down from 40 to 39 to 38. as the numbers counted down my curiosity of where that link will take me began to grow i hovered the mouse over the box then stopped myself what if clicking this link would install some virus onto my computer i reached for the top of my screen and began to close it what if it was the FBI trying to bait me into clicking a link to an illegal website just as the screen was about to meet my keyboard i stopped what if it really was a once in a lifetime opportunity and by clicking this link i would get the chance to view something no one has ever seen before the thought of never knowing where that link would take me is going to drive me crazy and i could surely see myself losing sleep over it i slowly lifted my laptop screen again and saw the numbers count down from five to four to three and click the link just as the timer reached one a new tab appeared on my screen as would look like a video began buffering do i blinked in confusion as all i saw was a very dark video feed with a blinking red dot in the corner of the screen next to the words life i stared at it for a few seconds trying to make out what exactly i was supposed to be looking at it appeared to be the shape of someone's silhouette did the link bring me to a live stream chat with some random person hello hello hello hello can you hear me can you hear me you hear me you hear me the person on the other end of the stream just sat there as i heard my voice echo for my computer speakers it kind of sounded like when you're on the phone with someone and they have their volume turned up so you can hear your voice repeating while you're talking to them i sat there for a full minute not saying anything waiting for the person in the live stream to respond or move or do pretty much anything they just sat there the whole time barely moving then from the corner of the screen i saw another figure standing in the background at first the second figure just stood there unmoving then began to sway back and forth the figure behind no longer seemed human its movement was just too strange and unnatural this continued for another minute then it stopped and went rigid its head began to twitch to the side every so often becoming faster and more rapid the other figure just sat there motionless as if unaware of what's going on behind it i then shifted my gaze to the figure behind as it began to slowly walk closer and closer to the person sitting closest to the screen who still to this moment just sat there motionless just staring at the screen my heart began to race why don't they notice what's going on are they drugged is this some kind of prank or some sick film being streamed on the dark web by some psychopath i wanted to yell out to that person warning them of the figures standing dangerously close to them whose movement was no doubt not human god i wish that the image was more clear just when i thought it was about to be all over the twitching figure stopped then slowly began to crouch down off camera and i could no longer see it from behind the seated figure in front of the screen after my heart began to slow down i leaned in closer to the screen to try to get a better view of the mysterious figure in front of me then to my surprise the seated figure leaned in as well this guy's mimicking me i then noticed a small light at the top of my computer monitor a steady green light it was then i noticed that my camera lens was extremely dusty it's a wonder that the fecker on the other end could not even see me i reached my sleeve up and gently wiped the dust off the monitor camera second my gaze returned to my screen i felt my heart begin to race the figure i've been staring at this whole time was me this whole live stream was not a two-way video chat it was just a recording of me sitting in front of my laptop then just like that the image disappeared from the screen my mind raised as everything began to settle in if this was a recording of me that means that the figure behind was a recording as well i made two mistakes that night the first was clicking that link and the second was looking under my table

CHAPTER FOUR

Exam preparation

this incident happened to me one year ago our final exams were coming up and I still needed to do a lot more preparation usually our schools library would close by 5:00 but because of the exams the school decided that the library would be kept open until midnight so that if kids wanted they could stay to study and prepare for the exams my house wasn't far away from the school so instead of studying at home I preferred studying in the quiet calm library and mostly prepared for the exams there that day I left my house at 6 o clock and soon reached the library to prepare for the exams I was so absorbed in studying I didn't realize that it was now 10 o'clock I had never stayed in the library for that long usually I would be on my way home at around 8 even at 8 o clock there would be at least some students in the library but at 10 there was absolute silence I only had about 10 to 15 minutes of work left so I decided I'll just finish this quickly and then return home I was completely lost in my work when I heard someone limping I quickly grabbed my books and ran out of the library there's a very long corridor outside our school library at the end of that corridor when you turn right you'll find the school exit door I went through the corridor and was quickly getting near the exit when I saw women standing at the end of that corridor I didn't know who she was but as I got nearer I felt more and more uncomfortable I got so uncomfortable that I called out who's there as soon as I said that she was gone within a few seconds I sighed a breath of relief and continued out the front door due to exhaustion and hunger I couldn't even walk properly but I noticed that the street was strangely completely empty which was extremely odd because the street is normally very busy even at night you can see people walking on the street DJ panic in fear I kept looking at the ground while walking I was nearly home when suddenly I saw a shadow on the ground stretching out to me even though there was no one around me when I lifted my head I saw a woman walking in front of me I found her very strange she looked as if she was disabled and that she was having trouble walking and she was walking so slowly that I caught up to her in no time now I was so close to her that I could see her clearly she was wearing tattered dirty clothes and her hands and feet were twisted also her hair looked very messy I found it so strange that I stopped in my tracks my gut was telling me over and over not to go any closer to this woman I didn't even have the courage to overtake her and walk on I was frozen I couldn't utter a word due to shock my brain went numb I didn't know how to answer her strange question out of fear I pointed far far away to the woman over there I just wanted her to go away she lived to where I had pointed to her and she walked so far away that I couldn't see her anymore I was terrified of the thought that she might appear in front of me again so I ran as fast as I could at that point my brain couldn't think about anything else other than finding someone who could help me a car or person or anyone and then at that moment I heard that woman screaming from far away yeah after that I remember nothing when I became conscious I found out that my neighbour found me passed out on the ground and he brought me home I found aside from him that in 1998 there was a 32 year old women named Agatha she had a 10 year old daughter who also went to Eden Hill school one day while playing with her friends she had an accident and died Agatha couldn't bear the thought of losing her after that Agatha's goes to a scene roaming around in Eden Hills CO and the surrounding area looking for her lost child she's still wandering hoping to be reunited with her daughter once again.

CHAPTER FIVE

Sleep Paralysis

when I was 19 years old in 1985 on New Year's Eve a bunch of my friends and I went to a rooftop bar of a hotel about a half hour before midnight I ran down to my car because I had forgotten my camera I figured I would have plenty of time to get back up there and find my friends I grabbed my camera and I got into an elevator all by myself about halfway up the elevator started shaking and it stopped completely I was trapped I have always had a problem with confined spaces so this was not an ideal situation for me after a few minutes everything went silent that was going on outside then out of nowhere the elevator lights went out and I started to hear children laughing but this was not the type of place where children would be my heart started beating faster and faster and harder and harder then all of a sudden I passed out as I woke up I noticed that I could not move or talk I thought to myself not sleep paralysis again then the lights started to flicker on and off and then all of a sudden I see a black figure to the left of me in the corner of the elevator crouching down smiling at me I tried to scream but nothing would come out I tried to move but I couldn't a guy came over the loudspeaker and told me there was an electrical short and that he would have me out soon there's a camera in the elevator so to the security yard it looked like I was just laying there I guess they figured I was drunk being that it's New Year's anyways every attempt to scream or move that figure would just start laughing at me and pointing this whole time the lights are flickering and all of a sudden I can hear the huge crowds counting down for New Year's 10 the dark figure is staring at me and now with a menacing smile with ten fingers up nine he's still looking at me with nine fingers up he's moving closer eight he was still looking at me with eight things up he's closer seven the same thing six the same thing five the same thing for he's drooling and he's much closer three he's closer to he was closer then the lights quit flickering and it was pitch black then all of a sudden outside when silent again I felt breathing in my right ear and then out of nowhere I hear one I couldn't breathe the lights started to flicker again then a figure was on my chest and all of a sudden it was gone and I can talk and move again usually when I have sleep paralysis something bad happens once I got out of the elevator an hour later I found out that there was a broad during the countdown on the rooftop bar that I was at and four people were killed by some maniac who was waiting until the end of the countdown and started hacking up people with a machete ever since then I have not had a sleep paralysis.

CHAPTER SIX

Pizza Delivery

I lived in a city in central Ohio that begins with SC and has a big college that I lived near I attended a different college than the one I mentioned and made the 20-minute drive from the city to that college I also worked nights as a pizza delivery man in the city and the surrounding suburbs one night I had an order in the town where my college is located which is a smaller suburban city northwest of my home city now this call occurred during what my coworkers are now referred to as the dead hour which is just before the shop closed at 1:00 in the morning I begrudging Lee took the pizzas got in the car and played the address into the GPS I noticed that the house was located off on a back road and what looked like a sparsely populated area not thinking much of this I drove up throughout 3:15 to I to 70 East and exited after passing through downtown the cemetery and the college I drove through some sub developments and then onto a smaller Road where the house was located the GPS notified me that I had arrived to my destination but to my surprise the house was boarded up I noticed that there was a small shed in the back of the house that had a small window there was a flickering light in the window at this point almost every red flag had gone off in my head but I knew my hard-ass boss will be pissed if I went down on this delivery so I proceeded towards the shed as I got closer to the shed I heard a rustling in the bushes next to the driveway and I heard a man whisper through the Khumbu 4444 at that point the man jumped out of the bushes and two other men jumped out of the shed they were carrying knives and were wearing these long ropes and white masks I made it back to the car just in time one of the assailants managed to slip my arm as I escaped I could see the assailant standing in the middle of the road looking pissed it probably drove 90 miles per hour I got to the shot everyone looked shocked after explaining everything to them we contacted the police and we dispatched a few officers to the house when they got bored the assailants were gone they found some drug paraphernalia in the shed and some ropes and some weird torture equipment.

CHAPTER SEVEN

Road Trip

I was on a road trip with my friend Tom throughout upstate New York on our second night of driving we were taking some peaceful back road through the woods because we were tired of the noisy highway so as we were driving down this narrow dilapidated road Tom suddenly really needed to use the bathroom I asked him if he could hold it but he said that if he held it any longer and his bladder would explode so I just sighed and tried to find like a gas station or something there was nothing to be seen though so I was thinking about pulling over and letting him piss in the woods but finally I saw lights cutting through the darkness of the head it was a 7-eleven thank God before I'd even part the car talking about the door and raced inside I realized while waiting in the dome I was actually hungry so I brought out some change from my pocket the way to least be enough for a bag of crabby Cheetos or something so then I went inside as I was walking through the store examining everything on the shelves I felt a tingly feeling on my neck like I was being watched I turned around and saw a bearded man in a yellow suit casually slip into the other aisle I rolled my eyes picked up a bag of cheez-its purchased them and walked out I looked back to my car looking at the dark woods behind the 7-eleven Tom had been gone forever so I texted to him and he told me he was just finishing taking a huge ship which was classic Tom I was just crunching on my cheese that's when I heard somebody cool I quickly looked around but saw nobody finally I spotted a man peeking his head around a tree in the dark woods his face was all dirty and he had glassy eyes we stood staring at each other for what seemed like the longest time until he said hell no I got in my car and locked the doors tasting Tom to hurry the up I told him that was a creepy weirdo outside the car and he was all like I had be right over later on he walked out the doors and climbed into the car and I hit the gas to get as far away from that place as possible as we were driving I looked back one last time in the rear-view mirror and saw three cloaked bulky men standing in the trees surrounding the 7-eleven needless to say I still have no idea what the hell was going on at that place nor do I have a lot to find out.

CHAPTER EIGHT

Camping Alone

my name is Yousef on 21 years old a few weeks ago my parents decided to go to Lebanon for a few days while I stayed home I was happy to have a few days to myself so I decided to drive to the light which my family when I was small it was remote surrounded by trees and barely anyone goes there I decided to stay for one night though as I got there I decided to dare myself into skinny-dipping since I was alone the be honest was quite refreshing and relaxing as it was getting dark I took out some firewood to try out with a campfire and got my lunch that night I dared myself into sleeping naked under my towel as I will never get another chance like this as I woke up I was shocked my towel was gone I couldn't find my clothes either I felt scared that's this man I wasn't alone in the woods to my luck my car keys were his total so I decided to get home however since I was staying for one night I didn't bring any extra clothes due to my condition I had to drive on those barely rose to avoiding exposure there was a bumpy ride but it was worth it after a few hours I saw men in vistas in your de Road he tripped and hit his head with rock despite my condition I knew I needed to stop and give him some help but as I saw him I realized he was wearing the same clothes I were yesterday I got out to ask if he's okay but he didn't move as I got closer he grabbed my hand and looked at me he had wide eyes and a huge terrifying smile I was more scared than I like to admit I quickly got in my car and drove away I managed to get home by sunset and took me a few minutes that of all who want my front door I have no return to the lake and his smile haunted me ever since you.

CHAPTER NINE

The Girl

my name is caitlin this incident happened when i was 14 years old and i will never forget this memory one day i was at home alone at my house my mom was still at the office late at night and my two siblings were at my grandparents house which was kind of far away from my home at first i was just enjoying my time alone watching netflix and doing some fun stuff however after a while i got pretty bored so i decided to invite some of my friends over i asked my mom for permission and then called my friends to invite them over a few moments later while i was waiting for them i heard a loud bang upstairs i was sure that there was no one else upstairs so i stood up and looked up the stairs with an anxious look on my face when i was near the stairs i could see that one of my dolls had fallen i picked it up and when i straightened my back something caught my attention a little girl was standing upstairs well i could feel that she was staring at me even though i couldn't see her face clearly due to the darkness i was terrified and then someone rang the doorbell i ran to see who it was and luckily my friends had arrived thank god it was a moment of relief that my friends came over at the right time soon i got my mind off of the girl i saw we sat down in the living room and had fun talking with each other an hour later one of my friends suggested that we should take some pictures together so we gathered around one another we took several selfies while laughing and chatting later as we scrolled through the pictures we found something there was a little girl standing behind our couch what made us even more terrified was the fact that she had no face i mean her face was just an empty darkness no eyes no nose and no mouth being terrified i told cassie to delete that picture right away however she said that something was wrong with her cell phone i snatched the phone out of her hands and tried to delete it but no matter what we tried we couldn't delete the picture then we heard loud thumps it sounded like someone's footsteps were coming from upstairs and our light was flickering on and off at the same time we thought that we couldn't stay inside anymore so we rushed outside in a hurry one of my friends Christina suddenly pointed at my bedroom window and said that there was someone in there i raised my eyes up and followed her finger and there she was it was the same faceless girl we had seen in the picture my friends and i screamed i called my mom and explained everything my mom couldn't believe what i told her so she made me calm down and said that she would be home in five minutes after she arrived home she searched the entire house but she couldn't find any trace of the girl i hoped that it was just our imaginations however we soon decided to move out of the house because i kept seeing the girl after that incident we finally moved and from then on my mom never wanted me to be home alone so i always stayed with my siblings i still have no clue why the girl haunted me but i think it was because she wanted us to get out of the house well I'm just glad that i don't see that girl in my new house this happened to me while i was on my way home one night i was living in an apartment at the time when i arrived on the first floor of my building there was a piece of paper hanging on the wall that said that the elevator was out of service no not again i said to myself i lived on a pretty high floor so without any other choice i had to walk up the stairs i was walking up the stairs out of sheer desperation and all of a sudden i heard something then i began to feel uneasy i knew that crimes often occurred around my neighbourhood especially targeting people who were alone when i listened closely i could hear a pair of men's shoes and a pair of women's high heels walking at the same time i assumed that it was a couple you guys are having a hard time like me I'm struggling to walk up the stairs especially this late at night i thought to myself i sighed with relief and turned my head around however i will never forget what i saw at that moment there was a man who was crawling with a pair of men's shoes on his feet and a pair of high heels on his hands he was crawling towards me this happened a few years ago in the neighbourhood i grew up in when i was around six years old there was an incident where an old man who lived right in front of my house was murdered by a robber not only did the robber steal all his money but he also stabbed him brutally with a knife and then ran away according to the police the crime scene was as horrible as it sounds and unfortunately to this day the robber still hasn't been caught when they moved the old man's dead body and passed by my house my mom covered my eyes with her hands so that i wouldn't see it nevertheless i could see my neighbour's face through the gap between my mom's fingers after that even after a few months had passed the old man's house wasn't sold it was because there were a few strange rumours spreading around the neighbourhood about his house some said that people would always hear the old man's coughing and sobbing coming from inside whenever it rained ten years later all of the people who moved into his house had to leave and now his house is being used as a warehouse when i was in high school i was crazy about a boy band and used to stay up late at night watching their videos because of this i used to fall asleep at around 3 or 4 AM the town i lived in was sort of a new city under construction so it was really quiet and there was no one outside during that time one night it was around three a.m i suddenly heard a woman singing outside it was an old song and the strange thing was that the woman was singing just one part of the song over and over again she didn't move on to the next section she would just start singing pause for a minute and then continued singing again out of curiosity i opened the window and was about to sing the next verse of the song to surprise her however before that i sent a text message to my friend hey someone is singing outside and keeps repeating the same part lol should i sing along with her not long after my friend responded and then i had to shut the window quietly because i was terrified the text said don't do that that's a ghost when ghosts find someone to harm they first sing and then wait .

CHAPTER TEN

The Carpenter At My House

this happened not long after we moved into our house in 2003 it was a nice and big house which was made in the 1950s one day i was in my backyard watering the grass and then out of the corner of my eye i saw something that made me pause there was a man standing next to the shrubs near our backyard's wall he was dressed like a carpenter his head looked like it was tilted sideways and his body was slightly facing our fences sideways then he saw me and smiled kindly at me at first i thought he was fixing someone's house and that it was his job however only after he faced me i realized that wasn't the case when i looked at him with narrowed eyes i noticed that his neck was visibly broken causing his head to awkwardly tilt to the side i then saw that he waved at me once but i was too shocked to scream at the time after i regained consciousness i looked around but he had vanished and had literally faded away two nights later i woke up at 3AM noise was coming from my ceiling it sounded like someone wearing construction boots was walking very slowly i started to freak out thinking that it might be a thief however i suddenly realized that that part of the roof was so thin which meant nobody could walk on it the steps abruptly stopped after a while and when i felt at ease i heard another horrible sound i heard a sharp scream that sounded like a man then a loud thud as if someone had dropped on my ceiling followed after i covered my head with a blanket my hands and whole body shivered and after 10 minutes of nothing i peeked outside it was completely quiet i saw and heard nothing but i couldn't fall back asleep that night the next morning i started to look up the history of the house to my surprise it turned out that there was a report about the carpenter i met a few days before in the backyard in 1958 he had been hired to fix the roof while the owners were on vacation however the carpenter had fallen abruptly through the weak spot on the roof while he was working and had broken his neck he couldn't scream for help and no one ever knew what happened to him as the owners were gone for two weeks he was finally found when they came back but had already died this happened right above my bedroom suddenly i felt bad for the poor guy and i guess he's still looking after things since then I've seen him sometimes but I'm no longer afraid of him.

CHAPTER ELEVEN

I can't believe my eyes

this story is about when i first moved to the city and joined the company our company was running a dormitory at the time and i was the one from the countryside so i decided to stay in the dormitory one day after work i came back to the dormitory and was eating my dinner with the TV on it was almost midnight after working overtime i was laughing and watching some comedy shows and then i felt a sudden strangeness you know like it feels like someone is staring at you feeling weird i turned my head toward the window and i couldn't move as my whole body stiffened with a tremendous chill i couldn't even scream the woman's face was stuck in the window as i turned casually to look and she was staring at me without any movement now let's think about it the windows in the dorm were not even small it was just the size of a normal person's upper body but look a face big enough to fill that size of a window can you imagine what it was and what was scarier was i was on the fifth floor at the time how could she even stand over there staring at me i was frozen i couldn't run away i could only just watch your glaring eyes it was lucky that i could move as the ghost disappeared the moment someone knocked on my door one of my co-workers in the next room came to my room saying that he had something urgent to do and when he looked at my pale face he asked me if i was okay so i explained to him what i had just saw and then his face looked a little stiff well he didn't say anything anymore but i knew it i was sure I'm not the only one who saw her here anyway something strange has happened to me since then sometimes when people get together and talk about ghost stories i suddenly start to feel nauseous like ghosts are coming to see me for example one day i was with my friends in a restaurant and as soon as they started talking about ghosts my skin turned pale and i started sweating all over my body at first they thought i was lying or trying to prank them but when i looked at the door with a serious look on my face and told my friends not to keep telling those stories they all had to shut up i think something's wrong with me anyone who's watching this story i hope you guys always check out the window especially when you're alone in your house always.

CHAPTER TWELVE

Granny

i used to live with my grandmother who died a few years ago my grandmother had suffered a cerebral infarction during her lifetime so she couldn't use her arms or legs at all and she couldn't even speak she could only mumble and grunt because i spent a lot of time with my grandmother i felt sorry for her whenever i saw her one day my family gathered together at my house to celebrate a big holiday while we were eating delicious food and chatting with each other my grandmother was sitting alone in her room a few hours had passed and it was time for everyone to go home so my relatives said their goodbyes however my grandmother was still in her room at that time so i stayed with her i sat next to her you know just in case grandma do you want to go outside and say goodbye to everyone i asked looking at her face then grandma slowly turned her head towards me and opened her mouth i'm embarrassed at that instant i couldn't believe that she spoke with such clear and accurate pronunciation a few years later after my grandma had died i told my family what happened that day when i was at the funeral hall but no one believed me today i'm going to talk about a story that i read somewhere a few years ago a body was found in the countryside it was especially difficult to identify the victim or the perpetrator of that incident because the body had been dead for quite a long time and to make matters worse the bones had changed and were bleached however the police found one strange thing in this difficult situation only one finger from its body remained completely intact they asked the national forensic service and they finally completed the identification on the body's finger furthermore they succeeded to arrest the criminal as a result of the investigation it turned out that the assailant was her roommate they said that he beat her to death on a rainy day and buried her in the mountain behind their house after that the detective who was in charge said in his interview when you're in charge of a case there are often things that occur that can't be explained however i can tell you that ghosts really exist i'll admit that what i'm about to tell you is not that creepy my grandmother passed away not too long ago after staying three days in the funeral home we were supposed to go to the cemetery following her cremation they said it would take about an hour so my mom told me to take a nap in the car until the cremation was done since i was the one who had to drive later i went back to my car alone and fell asleep however not long after someone started shaking me i heard my name so i slowly opened my eyes and my grandmother was sitting next to me grandma i asked rubbing my eyes and she smiled at me yes it's me your grandpa is calling me i'll go first so stop sleeping and get up i really missed her crying in my dream i suddenly woke up with a surge of longing for her i kept crying and then came out of the car at that moment i saw my family walking towards me carrying a box of grandmother's ashes and her picture i immediately told my mom about my dream and then she patted me on the back and said this i guess grandma wanted to say goodbye before she left maybe you were the only one who was sleeping so she wanted to say goodbye to you.

CHAPTER THIRTEEN

True old building

one evening i was looking for internet cafe because i needed to send a few emails i spotted one in the old building the sign said it was on the sixth floor when i walked through the entrance there was a dark hallway that led to a small elevator i pressed the call button and when the doors open i stepped inside in a lot of asian countries many buildings do not have a fourth floor the number four is considered bad luck because the word four sounds almost the same as the word for death when it stopped and the doors open i was about to step out when i realized that something was wrong the hallway was in total darkness by the lighting mounting from the elevator i could make out a random piece of furniture covered with white cloth it looked like it hadn't been touched in years i thought i might have gotten off on the wrong floor so i checked the buttons but none of them were lit up there was nothing to indicate which floor i was on just then i noticed something moving at the end of the darkened hallway i couldn't quite make out what it was but it looked like a person dressed in some type of gown the figure was moving slowly down the hallway towards the elevator they creeped me out in a panic i started pressing the closed door button all of a sudden the light in the elevator flickered and turned off i was plunging to the pitch darkness i was so freaked out i almost wet myself just as i was about to lose it completely the lights flickered back on the doors closed the elevator jolted back to life and began to ascend again i breathed a sigh of relief when the doors opened this time i was at the internet cafe i went over to the counter and told the girl who worked there and what had happened as she listened her face grew pale she said that some of the customers and a few of her co-workers had experienced the same thing she had never experienced anything herself but she told me about the history of the building apparently the fourth floor had been a hair salon at one time it was prospering and doing pretty good until one of the women who worked there killed herself in the salon nobody knew the reason why the salon continued to operate but they were plagued by weird and inexplainable events sometimes when customers were having their hair washed the water were turned as red as blood other people claimed that when they looked in the mirror they would catch glimpses of a ghostly figure standing behind them when they turned around there would be no one there because of these events the salon developed a bad reputation and began to lose customers eventually they were forced to close down the building's owner tried to rent the fourth floor out to other businesses but when they found out what had happened nobody would take it finally the owner reduced the price to nearly nothing and it was rented by a businessman who planned to open a stationary supply store however when they tried to do some renovations on the floor there was a series of mysterious accidents the workman's tools would sometimes disappear only to be found in the strange places a large mirror suddenly shattered when nobody was near it and the workman had his hand crushed when the elevator closed unexpectedly eventually the workmen were so spooked that they refused to continue the building's owner gave up trying to rent the fourth floor out and just shut it down he had the buttons and the elevator replaced and it was reprogrammed that nobody could go on the fourth floor at least that's what's supposed to happen for some reason when people took the elevator it would sometimes stop on the fourth floor and when the doors open some people would see a figure coming toward them i honestly still don't know what that was.

CHAPTER FOURTEEN

The old lady I met in my dream

when i was a little girl i had the same dream several times in these dreams i used to see an old lady who kept running after me she was wearing korean traditional clothes called a handbook and put her white hair up whenever it happened she was kind of far away from me so i tried to run away from her at full speed but then when i turned my head around in less than three seconds she had already reached me and was right behind me with an angry look on her face and stretching out her hand so i always woke up crying when i felt like i was going to get caught by her that horrible situation repeated over and over again whenever i had a dream however the interesting thing was that i never got caught by her in my dream because i was so young at the time it was really scary to see that old lady in my dream so i tried to not fall asleep but eventually i couldn't win and sleep took over my body and the same thing happened again in one dream i was playing at the playground with my older brother we were playing with some dirt and i could see the old lady watching us as usual to be more specific she was staring at me run hurry as soon as i told him that she ran towards us but this time she looked even more angry than usual i was in a hurry so i yelled at my brother to go up on the slide and we both ran towards it i was going to go up the slide but suddenly i stumbled and fell down as she was approaching i was about to scream but to my surprise she just passed me and then she angrily grabbed my brother's leg with one hand and pulled him downwards being terrified i cried and yelled at her to let go of him and then i suddenly woke up when i woke up i realized that my whole body was drenched in cold sweat a few days later an unforgettable and unbelievable incident happened to me my brother was in a car accident not to mention his teeth cheekbones ribs right leg and shoulders were all smashed it was just horrible but since the accident i couldn't stop thinking of the old lady who I'd met in my dream well it's been a long time now but i still remember her face so vividly since my brother's accident the old lady was no longer in my dreams however to this day i'm still really curious why did the old lady appear in my dream and what did she want to say to me.

CHAPTER FIFTEEN

The unforgivable mistake

I'm someone who goes on a deep and dark web constantly it's not what people think words evil and overpopulated with crazy people that's only a small percentage of the dark web years ago my girlfriend broke up with me and i put her personal information on the forum and soon after that she disappeared it's been a while since that happened and i've ran into people that have disrespected me since i'm not an intimidating guy nor do i look intimidating nor do i ever have physical or verbal conflicts i always think to myself that these people don't know what could happen to them i work at a fast food restaurant and at the time of this story my manager was really on my case about everything i would be late mess up orders have an attitude with customers and some other stuff i could name but it's so much i understood that i was messing up but the tone that this guy would talk to me embarrassed me in front of my co-workers and sometimes in front of customers one day though that was the last straw so one day i walked into work five minutes before i was due to clock in and my manager out loud said that the window liquor is finally on time in front of customers and my co-workers everyone laughed at me during my whole shift at night he would direct smart comments toward me while still yelling at me for everything that i did wrong i made up my mind i was going to find that forum and give his information on my walk home i was going back and forth with myself about whether to do it or not by the time i made it home i made up my mind i didn't shower nor did i change clothes i went straight to my laptop and i searched i possibly clicked maybe a hundred links because on the dark web there are links that will take you down any rabbit hole a link named porkchop piqued my interest when i clicked it i was directed to an about page it only says six words we find it we chop it and another link that said here's an example of what we do i clicked it of course as soon as i clicked on it the picture went to the point of view from an old school camera with the date and time in the corner of the screen the person behind the camera approached the man and followed him a few minutes go by and the man noticed what was happening he turned around and approached the camera while yelling and screaming at the person for following him then all of a sudden you see five huge guys dressed in black wearing a pig mask run from behind a man and drag him into the dark the person holding the camera turns the camera to his or hers face and leaves it there for about five to ten minutes that person also wore a pig mask but all you could hear was the man screaming and sounds that i don't want to describe in the background the camera was then turned back around and the sight that i saw was disturbing it was something that no one would ever want to see some people say that they wouldn't wish it on their worst enemy but i did after their video was over there were links one said pork and the other said chop i clicked on the pork and it prompted me to put in a cold i didn't have one so i backed out so i clicked on shop there was information that needed to be filled out like name height description in place i filled out all the info for my manager in a place it was my job i submitted the form at the end of the screen it said see you soon four days later while at work my manager approached me and decided to apologize for the way he treated me and offered to give me more hours and said that he will work with me more often because he sees potential in me a few hours later it was close to the end of the night my manager helped me with the trash and took it out for me as i were putting chairs on top of the table getting ready to mop i looked outside and saw my manager looking over at something but he looked worried i moved to get a better look and i saw what he was looking at he was surrounded by six people in a pig mask with weapons in her hands i ran outside as they swarmed him except for one person he had a camera i forgot all about these guys and then i put his information on the website i ran outside as they approached him he looked at me for help but i ran back inside and called the police it took them 10 minutes to get there when i look back outside what i saw was the most disgusting thing i've ever seen i wish i could get the image out of my head between the time of me initially seeing them calling the cops and running back outside these guys were gone but my manager was still there i went to his funeral the next week the next day i received an anonymous email that had the whole video they were watching him this whole time he was on shift i don't know how they got my email i never provided any of my information till this day i still feel sick because my manager was starting to be nice to me that day i can't go back on the dark.

CHAPTER SIXTEEN

Something Was Happening In My House

Way this happened over 25 years ago but the memories are still fresh on my mind i moved in with my boyfriend who was a musician and i wasn't working at the time our budget was small so when we were offered super cheap rent for our house we jumped at the opportunity it should have been a red flag at the time but we were in no position to refuse it was far from the city center we had almost no furniture and lived quite the frugal life but we were happy to have our own space the house was simple but cozy and nice and there was another room in the backyard with no windows but only a chair right in the middle of it needless to say it was super creepy so i avoided that part of the house while my boyfriend was working all day in a music school i took care of the house in the beginning everything was fine i felt happy there but after a few weeks weird things started happening one day i put some of the cans and ingredients on the kitchen table while i was cooking however when i turned around to grab them they weren't there at first i just thought that i had forgotten to pick them up from the shelves but when cans and knives started showing up in random places in the house like the bedroom i started paying more attention my boyfriend also experienced the same things and whenever he found the missing items he just laughed about it however things started to change and took a turn for the worse when we decided to clean the backyard we cut the grass threw away the trash and decided to move the chair in the middle of the room so my boyfriend picked it up and left it in front of the house to be collected he told me that he felt sick the moment he entered that room i thought he was overreacting but when i entered it i immediately felt a heavy weight on my chest and a piercing headache however everything would be fine again once we left that area it was scary so we went to a local church got some holy water and salt from the priest and cleaned the room we thought that everything would be okay now my boyfriend had to leave for work and i continued cleaning inside the house but i didn't feel calm and perky as i usually did because i constantly had the feeling that someone was watching me i even checked the doors and windows to see if there was anyone around but no one was there and i still felt uncomfortable and was paranoid all day when my boyfriend returned home in the evening we started hearing noises coming from outside this area was kind of dangerous especially at night so my boyfriend was super careful when going outside he thought that it could be a robbery everything was alright except for the fact that the chair was back inside the room it was in the same place as before so he got really mad when he saw it thinking that some punk was playing a trick on us he went outside and decided to grab the chair break it and throw it away but i could see the panic on his face when he couldn't move the chair for whatever reason it was completely fixed to the ground not like it was glued to the floor but more like it weighed 10 tons no matter how hard he tried it wouldn't move because he had to come up with another plan he ran inside grabbed holy water and salt made a circle around the chair and started praying suddenly we heard a loud bang thousands maybe millions of cockroaches started coming out of every sewer hole outside of the house i am terribly terrified of cockroaches so i guess this was my worst nightmare he left the chair and we rushed inside the house and after we checked everywhere in the house we locked all the doors and windows and then ran away to my mom's house as the incident happened on a friday evening we decided to stay at her house until sunday to calm down on sunday afternoon we returned home and everything fell to normal there were no traces of insects around and the chair was still in its place but the house seemed quiet we started relaxing a bit and as i had just refilled the fridge on friday with groceries i decided to start cooking something nice for dinner however when i opened the fridge i saw an image i will never forget all the food was full of maggots and it was almost completely decomposed the smell was horrible inside i have never seen anything like it before i mean the fridge was still on and seemed to be working but the food was not frozen and this level of decomposition could not be reached in less than 48 hours it was the most disgusting thing i've ever seen i screamed and showed it to my boyfriend who also couldn't understand what happened but there was nothing we could do with the food or the fridge later we finally decided to give the house back and we moved out to another city and fortunately i've never experienced anything like that again but that incident still gives me the chills.

9 798885 460439

Printed by Libri Plureos GmbH in Hamburg,
Germany